Dear Parent:
Your child's love of readin

Every child learns to read in a different way and at his or her own speed. Some go back and forth between reading levels and read favorite books again and again. Others read through each level in order. You can help your young reader improve and become more confident by encouraging his or her own interests and abilities. From books your child reads with you to the first books he or she reads alone, there are I Can Read Books for every stage of reading:

SHARED READING
Basic language, word repetition, and whimsical illustrations, ideal for sharing with your emergent reader

BEGINNING READING
Short sentences, familiar words, and simple concepts for children eager to read on their own

READING WITH HELP
Engaging stories, longer sentences, and language play for developing readers

READING ALONE
Complex plots, challenging vocabulary, and high-interest topics for the independent reader

ADVANCED READING
Short paragraphs, chapters, and exciting themes for the perfect bridge to chapter books

I Can Read Books have introduced children to the joy of reading since 1957. Featuring award-winning authors and illustrators and a fabulous cast of beloved characters, I Can Read Books set the standard for beginning readers.

A lifetime of discovery begins with the magical words **"I Can Read!"**

Visit www.icanread.com for information
on enriching your child's reading experience.

Meet the Dragons

I Can Read Book® is a trademark of HarperCollins Publishers.

How to Train Your Dragon: Meet the Dragons
How to Train Your Dragon ™ & © 2010 DreamWorks Animation L.L.C.
Library of Congress catalog card number: 2009937693
ISBN 978-0-06-156733-9

Typography by Rick Farley

10 11 12 13 14 LP/WOR 10 9 8 7 6 5 4 3 2 ❖ First Edition

DREAMWORKS

HOW TO TRAIN YOUR
DRAGON
Meet the Dragons

Adapted by Catherine Hapka
Pencils by Charles Grosvenor
Paintings by Justin Gerard

HARPER

An Imprint of HarperCollinsPublishers

Berk was a cold, harsh island.
The Vikings who lived there
had to fight to survive.

Who did the Vikings fight?

Dragons!

They were fierce beasts of all sizes.

Hiccup was a very small Viking.

His father, Stoick,

was a very large one.

Stoick was the proud leader

of the Viking village.

Hiccup invented weapons,
like the Mangler, to fight dragons.
Once he was pretty sure he hit
an attacking Night Fury!

With each attack, the dragons stole
more and more food.
Stoick ordered all of the adults
to sail off in search of
the dragons' island.

The teenagers had to learn

to defend Berk.

Astrid was a tough Viking girl

with her own axe.

She couldn't wait for dragon training.

The other teens were excited, too.

Ruffnut and Tuffnut were twins.

They were always competing

to see which of them

was rougher and tougher.

Shoutlout loved danger.

He was quick to act

and slow to think.

Fishlegs was a little more careful,

but he still liked to fight.

Gobber was the teens' teacher.
On the first day of training,
he brought out a stout dragon
called a Gronckle.

Gronckles could eat rocks
and turn them into lava balls.
They could hover and fly backward.
But they couldn't make fire
if their heads got wet.

Next Gobber showed them

a tiny dragon

called the Terrible Terror.

The Terrible Terror was the size
of a dog.

But it was no less deadly.

"When it comes to dragons,
size does not matter," Gobber said.

Next on the list
was the Deadly Nadder.
Nadders could breathe fire
and shoot darts from their tails.

But Nadders also had a weakness.

They had a blind spot.

If Hiccup stood still, he was safe

because the dragon could not see him.

The last dragon that Gobber showed
the group was the Hideous Zippleback.
It was the trickiest
of all the dragons.

Each Zippleback had two heads.

One head breathed explosive gas.

The other head lighted it.

Ka-boom!

After the first day of training,

Hiccup went for a walk

and found an injured Night Fury.

"I did it!" he realized.

"I brought down this mighty beast!"

The Night Fury
had lost part of his tail
when the Mangler hit him.

Hiccup secretly befriended
the dragon and named him Toothless.
Then he started doing his best
to replace the dragon's tail
with one of his inventions.

Soon Toothless could fly again!
The dragon took Hiccup
soaring through the sky.

One day Astrid followed Hiccup
when he went to visit Toothless.
She could hardly believe
what she saw.
Hiccup was friends with a dragon!

"What have you done?" she cried.

Then she ran toward the village

to tell the other Vikings.

Astrid didn't get very far.

Toothless grabbed her

and carried her to the top

of a very tall tree.

That gave Hiccup a chance to
explain.
He even talked Astrid
into climbing onto the dragon
for a ride.

Toothless flew through the clouds
with Hiccup and Astrid on his back.
Astrid could hardly believe it.
"He's amazing!" she cried.

Hiccup felt hopeful.

He knew that dragons

weren't as mean and evil

as the Vikings had always thought.

Hiccup just had to show the others that dragons could be their friends. Maybe then Vikings and dragons could live together in peace!